I LOVE YOU

A Rebus Poem

by JEAN MARZOLLO
Illustrations by SUSE MACDONALD

Cartwheel
B·O·O·K·S ®

SCHOLASTIC INC.

New York   Toronto   London   Auckland   Sydney
Mexico City   New Delhi   Hong Kong

Every 🐦 loves a 🌳

Every 🌼
loves a 🐝

Every

loves a

And

Every 🧦 loves a 👟

Every loves a BOO

Every 1 loves a 2

And

👁 ❤ U

Every 🪏 loves a 🪣

Every

loves a

Every 🌊 loves a 🐋

And

Every  loves a

Every loves a

Every 🕯 loves a 🎂

And

👁 ❤ u

Every bird loves a tree,
Every flower loves a bee,
Every lock loves a key,
And I love you.

Every sock loves a shoe,
Every ghost loves a boo,
Every 1 loves a 2,
And I love you.

Every shovel loves a pail,
Every monkey loves a tail,
Every wave loves a whale,
And I love you.

Every farmer loves a rake,
Every duck loves a lake,
Every candle loves a cake,
And I love you.